For our granddaughter, Mina Fern
—G.E.L.

For Regular-Size Jerry, Dr. Mrs. Jerry, and Jerry Jr.,
who aren't that great
—B.L.

For Katie, Leo, Honey, Maggie, and always, Cheryl
—M.W.

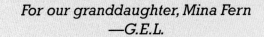

ATHENEUM BOOKS FOR YOUNG READERS
An imprint of Simon & Schuster Children's Publishing Division
1230 Avenue of the Americas, New York, New York 10020
Text copyright © 2019 by George Ella Lyon and Benn Lyon
Illustrations copyright © 2019 by Mick Wiggins
ATHENEUM BOOKS FOR YOUNG READERS is a registered trademark of Simon & Schuster, Inc.
Atheneum logo is a trademark of Simon & Schuster, Inc.
For information about special discounts for bulk purchases, please contact Simon & Schuster
Special Sales at 1-866-506-1949 or business@simonandschuster.com.
The Simon & Schuster Speakers Bureau can bring authors to your live event.
For more information or to book an event, contact the Simon & Schuster Speakers Bureau at
1-866-248-3049 or visit our website at www.simonspeakers.com.
Book design by Debra Sfetsios-Conover
The text for this book was set in Rockwell STD.
The illustrations for this book were rendered digitally.
Manufactured in China
0319 SCP
First Edition
10 9 8 7 6 5 4 3 2 1
Library of Congress Cataloging-in-Publication Data
Names: Lyon, George Ella, 1949- author. | Lyon, Benn, author. | Wiggins, Mick, illustrator.
Title: Trains run! / George Ella Lyon and Benn Lyon ; illustrated by Mick Wiggins.
Description: First edition. | New York : Atheneum Books for Young Readers, [2018] | "A Richard
Jackson Book." | Summary: Illustrations and simple, rhyming text reveal different kinds of
trains, how they run, and the sounds they make.
Identifiers: LCCN 2017035840| ISBN 9781481482028 (hardcover) | ISBN 9781481482035 (eBook)
Subjects: | CYAC: Stories in rhyme. | Railroad trains—Fiction.
Classification: LCC PZ8.3.L9893 Trf 2018 | DDC [E]—dc23
LC record available at https://lccn.loc.gov/2017035840

TRAINS RUN!

By George Ella Lyon and Benn Lyon

Illustrations By Mick Wiggins

A Richard Jackson Book

Atheneum · ATHENEUM BOOKS FOR YOUNG READERS · NEW YORK   LONDON   TORONTO   SYDNEY   NEW DELHI

Trains travel
down the track—
All day gone.
All night back.

Trains run!

chooka-c

Steam engine,
gas engine,
electric engine too.
Chooka-chooka! Vroom zoom!
Hssss! Whoo-oo-whoo!

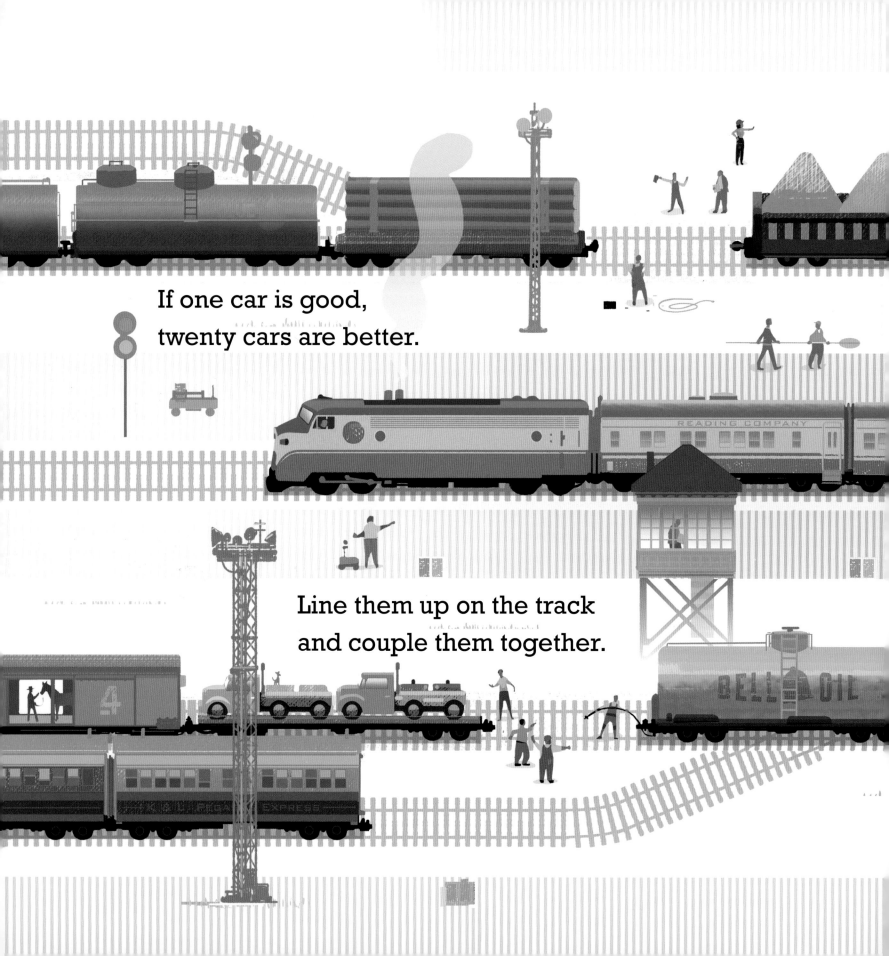

If one car is good,
twenty cars are better.

Line them up on the track
and couple them together.

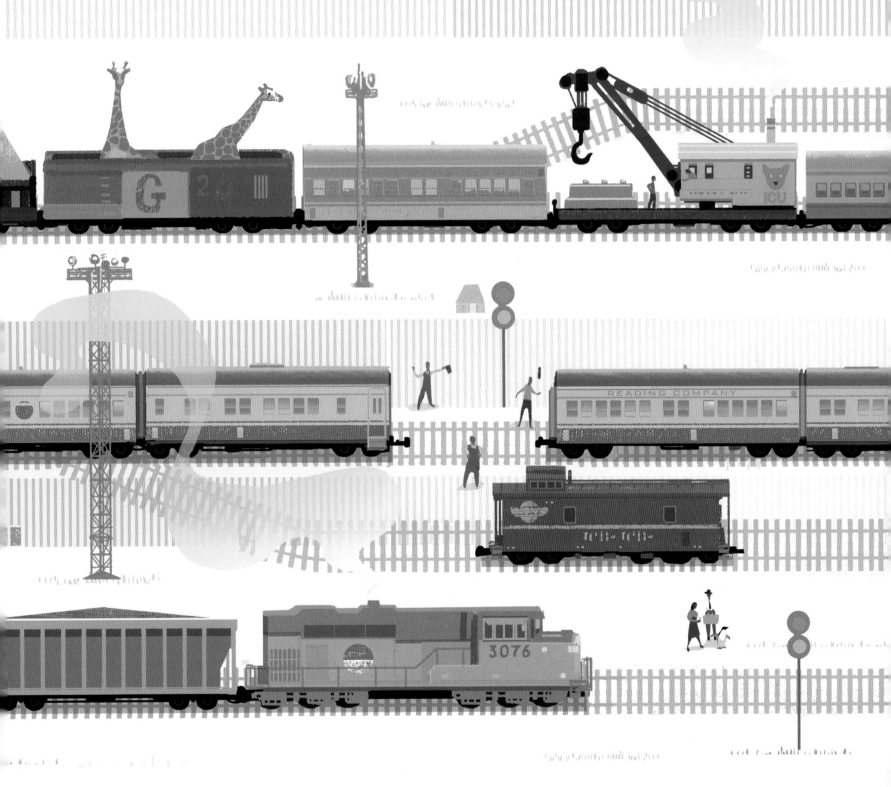

Trains run!

Boxcar, tank car,
lots of rolling stock.
Hurry up, workers!
Got to beat that clock!

On time,
down the line,
here comes Engine No. 9.

Trains run!

Locomotive,
so devoted,
pulls the cars
when they are loaded.

Iron horse
on its course
hauls the cars
with mighty force.

Toy train, circus train,
subway, or bullet—

Got to have an engine
to push it or pull it.

Steam engine,
gas engine,
electric engine too.
Chooka-chooka! Vroom zoom!
Hssss! Whoo-oo-whoo!

Railroad crossing. Signal flashing.
Down comes the gate.
Trains got to move on through.
Folks got to wait.

Trains run!

Trains go through snow

and jungles and sand.

Can a train climb a mountain?

I think it can!

Slow it goes up the slope,
fast across the bridge—
a long, strong trestle
that links ridge to ridge.

If the mountain's super high
the best way to do it
is to build a long tunnel
so the train can run through it.

Don't you want to try it?
Don't you want to ride
silver rails, train-track trails,
a friend by your side?

Buy your ticket at the station.
Find your platform, too.
Don't dillydally.
Trains won't wait for you.

Hear the cars rumble?
Hear the brakes wheeze?
It's your train rolling in.
"All aboard, please!"

hisss! whoo-

Steam engine,
gas engine,
electric engine too.
Chooka-chooka! Vroom zoom!
Hssss! Whoo-oo-whoo!

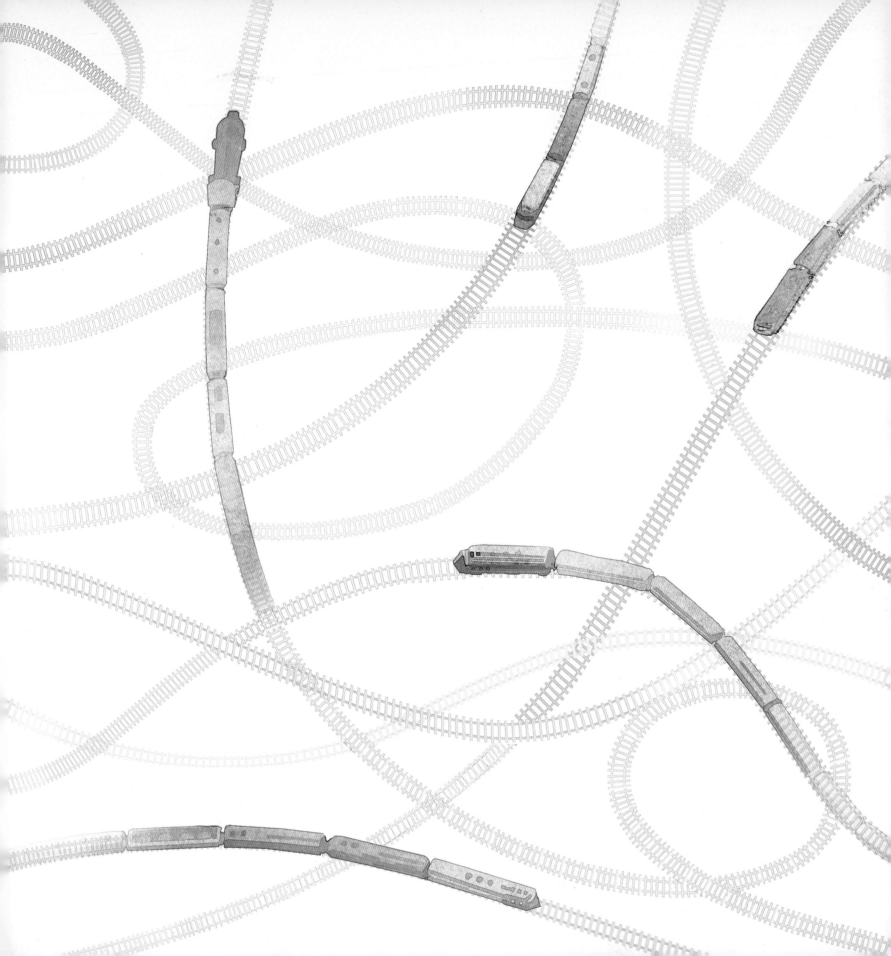